The Cupcake Princess

Teresa Gaydosz

Illustrated by Pamela Kate Hoffman

Archway Publishing books may be ordered through booksellers or by contacting:

Archway Publishing
1663 Liberty Drive
Bloomington, IN 47403
www.archwaypublishing.com
1 (888) 242-5904

Illustrations by Pamela Kate Hoffman

ISBN: 978-1-4808-1686-2 (sc)
ISBN: 978-1-4808-1687-9 (hc)
ISBN: 978-1-4808-1688-6 (e)

Print information available on the last page.

Archway Publishing rev. date: 6/1/2015

Dedicated to
Maren,
whose first breath was
amongst the angels

Once upon a time, there lived a princess in a not too distant land,
and unhealthy food to eat she would always demand.

"No, no, no!" she would scream and declare
when offered an apple, a carrot, or even a pear.

"I want instead...

1 vanilla iced cupcake

2 slices of pie just baked

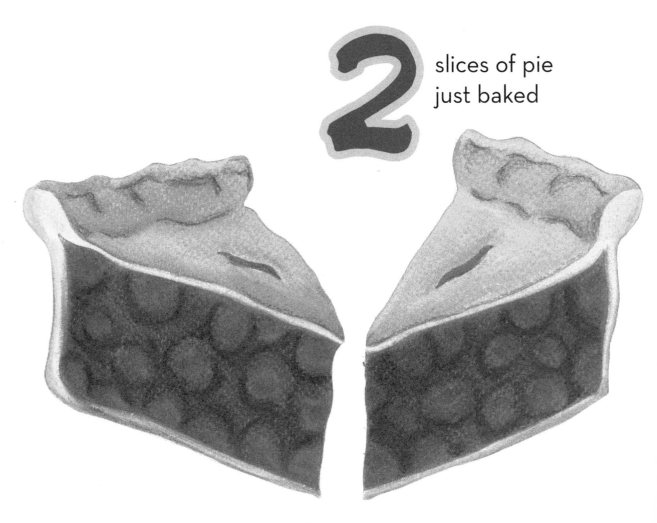

3 scoops of ice cream with cherry sauce on top

4 bottles of soda — pop, fizz, pop

5

5 pieces of
bubble gum in
colorful wrap

6 chocolate candies
to gobble in a snap

7 sugar cookies all
colorfully iced

8 donuts
would also
be nice

9 sweet lollipops each of various size

10 rainbow-colored gumdrops would delight the eyes

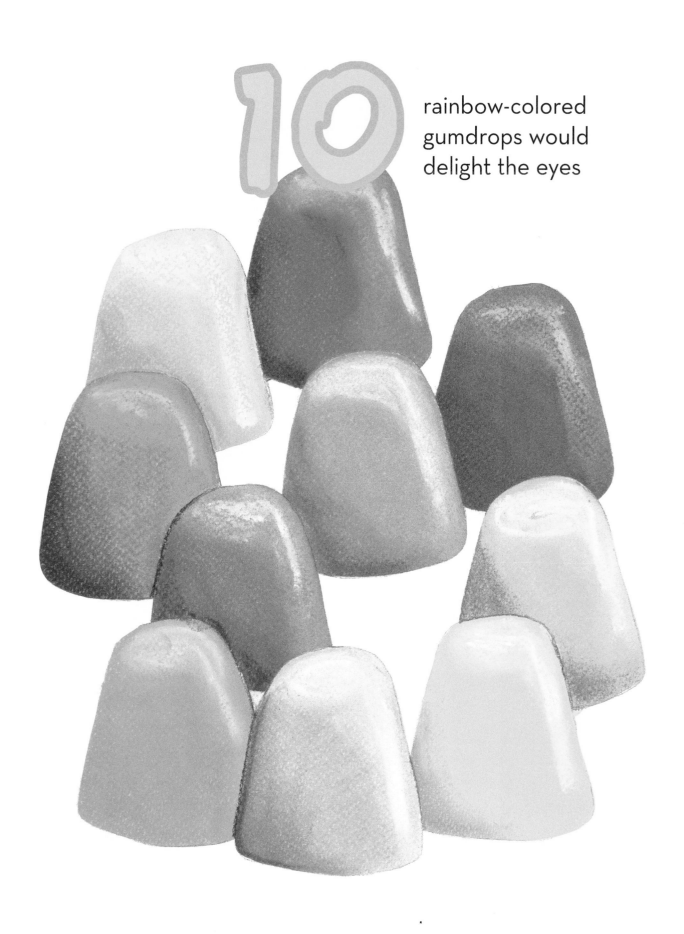

The castle chef was in despair.

"Boys and girls must eat
with wisdom and care!"

11

And before the princess
could scream and cry,

the chef offered her some
other foods to try.

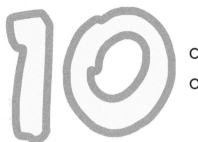 cucumber circles,
oh so green

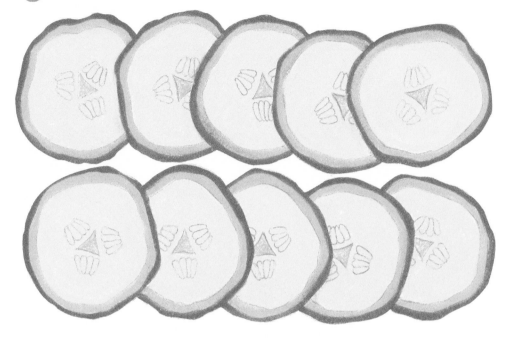

9 orange carrots to
keep you lean

14

8 crunchy celery
sticks here

7 long-stemmed
broccoli spears

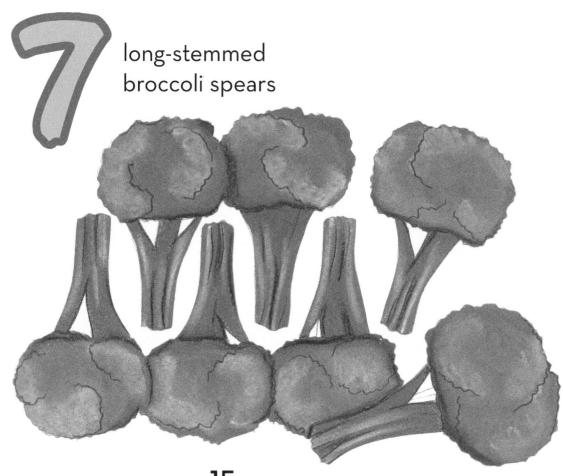

6 fresh strawberries from the field

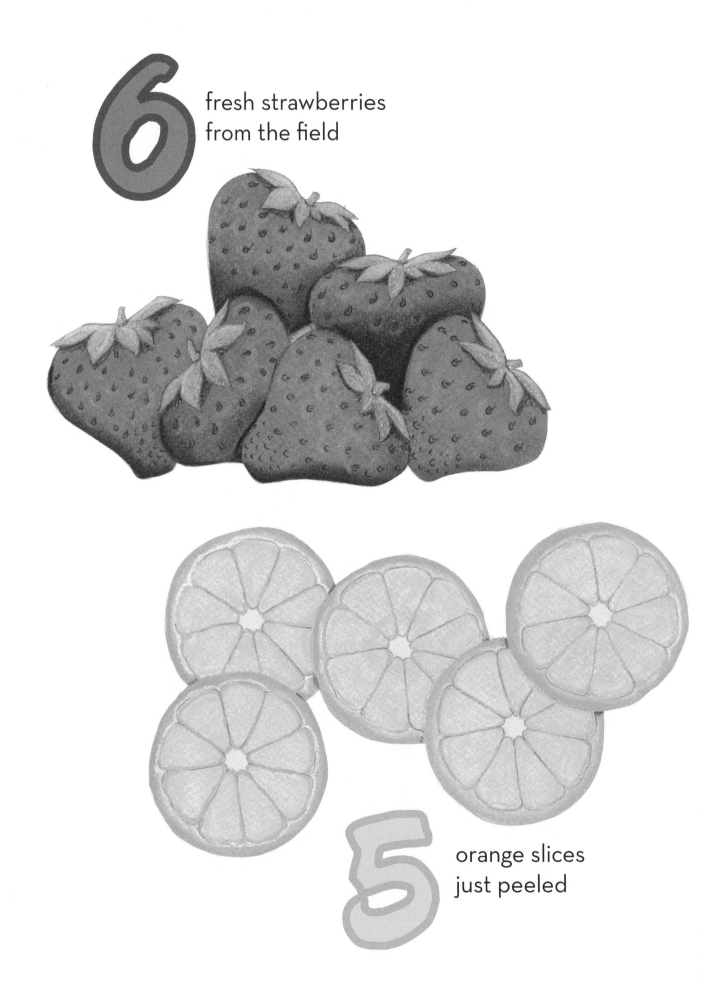

5 orange slices just peeled

4 raspberries bursting with flavor

3 pieces of kiwi to savor

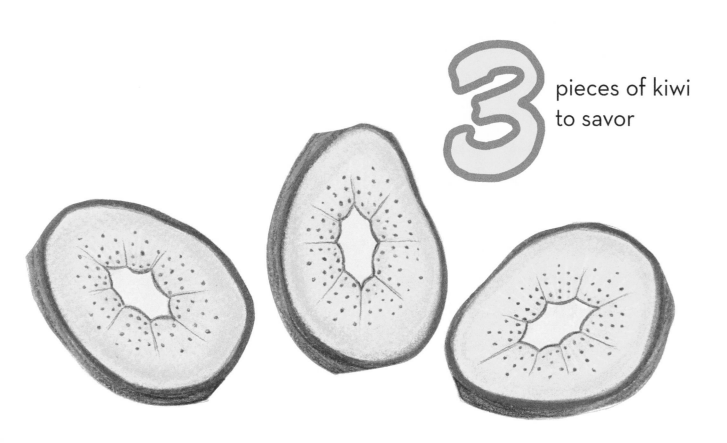

2 halves of a
peach to eat

1 juicy apple is
always a treat

The princess
tried the foods
with textures
so new.

She was surprised
with the delicious
tastes, too.

Vegetables and fruits are
some things she now tries.
And the little princess promised
to be healthy and wise.

But once in a while it is just fine...

THE END. ♡

CPSIA information can be obtained
at www.ICGtesting.com
Printed in the USA
BVHW02s1930250718
522610BV00017B/212/P

9 781480 816862